Callaghan, Jean Davis

Patty for president

Dear Parents:

Children learn to read in stages, and all children develop reading skills at different ages. **Ready Readers**™ were created to promote children's interest in reading and to increase their reading skills. **Ready Readers**™ are written on two levels to accommodate children ranging in age from three through eight. These stages are meant to be used only as a guide.

Stage 1: Preschool-Grade 1

Stage 1 books are written in very short, simple sentences with large type. They are perfect for children who are getting ready to read or are just becoming familiar with reading on their own.

Stage 2: Grades 1-3

Stage 2 books have longer sentences and are a bit more complex. They are suitable for children who are able to read but still may need help.

All the **Ready Readers**™ tell varied, easy-to-follow stories and are colorfully illustrated. Reading will be fun, and soon your child will not only be ready, but eager to read.

3 6990 00015 2447

Patty
for President

Written by Jean Davis Callaghan
Illustrated by Mary Ann Fraser

Modern Publishing
A Division of Unisystems, Inc.
New York, New York 10022

Pam and Patty are twins.

They are in the second grade.

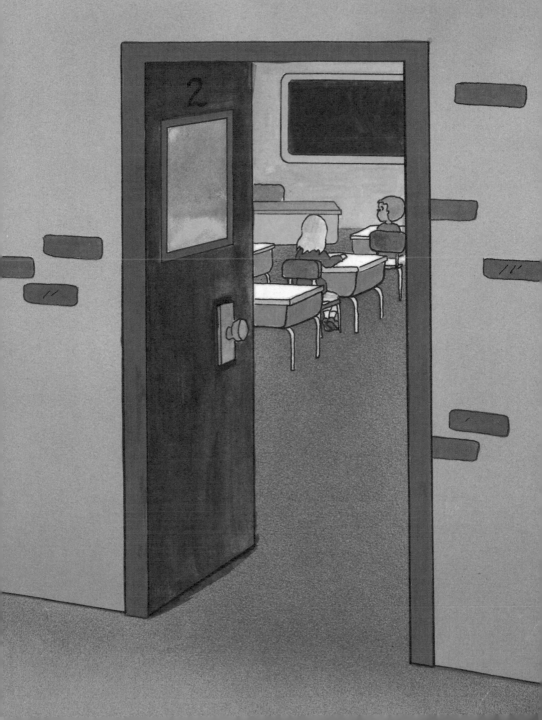

Friday, the class will vote
for the class president.

"Who will you vote for?"
Pam asks Patty.

"For myself," says Patty.
"I want to be president."

Patty tells everyone,
"Vote for me
for president."

Bossy Patty tells Pam,
"I want you to be my helper.
Go get some cookies
and pass them out.
Say they are from me."

"Also, I want you to help
everyone with their homework,
and tell them it was
my idea."

Pam doesn't like being bossed around, but she does love her sister.

So she bakes cookies and
hands them out to the class.

The class likes the cookies
so much, Patty asks Pam
to bring them every day.

During recess, and after school,
Pam helps the other students
with their homework.

It bothers Pam that Patty is so bossy, but Pam keeps working hard for her sister.

Pam works so hard that
she gets tired.
One day, she almost
falls asleep in class.

Patty doesn't do any work.
She only sits on the swing,
talking and laughing—

and eating the cookies
that Pam made.

Meanwhile, Pam works hard
to make Patty the second-grade
class president.

At last it is Friday.

The teacher says, "It's time for the class to vote."

Everyone waits to see who will get the most votes.

The teacher says, "The class president is…

...Pam!"

Pam wins because the class thinks she is a kind person, and a hard worker.